BK1 TRIPPIN'

PJ GRAY

SADDLEBACK
EDUCATIONAL PUBLISHING

BK1 TRIPPIN'

TRIPPIN': BOOK 1

THE ACCIDENT: BOOK 2

THE LAB: BOOK 3

SADDLEBACK
EDUCATIONAL PUBLISHING
www.sdlback.com

Copyright ©2015 by Saddleback Educational Publishing

ISBN-13: 978-1-62250-931-7
ISBN-10: 1-62250-931-5
eBook: 978-1-63078-052-4

Printed in the U.S.A.
0000/00-00-00

19 18 17 16 15   1 2 3 4 5

AUTHOR ACKNOWLEDGEMENTS

I wish to thank Carol Senderowitz for her friendship and belief in my abilities. Additional thanks and gratitude to my family and friends for their love and support; likewise to the staff at Saddleback Educational Publishing for their generosity, graciousness, and enthusiasm. Most importantly, my heartfelt thanks to Scott Drawe for his love and support.

JUST A HOUSE

Troy was in his last foster home. He hated it. Just like he hated all the others. His foster mom had many kids. She also had a job.

Troy would lie in bed at night. He would dream of leaving. He wanted a place of his own.

Troy began to skip school. He did not have friends. He liked to be alone.

He tried to stay out of fights. But if he had to fight, he would. And he tried to stay away from gangs. It was hard.

Troy had one more year of high school. His grades were bad and getting worse. He did not want to go back.

"The cops found you again," his foster mom said. "You were in the park. You have to stay in school."

"You can't make me go," Troy said.

"Fine! Don't go!" she yelled. "You can stay here. Take care of the kids. How about that?"

"No way!" Troy said.

"Then you better stay in school."

RUN AWAY

It was five in the morning. His foster mom was sleeping. The other kids were sleeping. Troy took some food and his clothes. He put them in a backpack.

Troy snuck out of the house. He stole his foster brother's bike. He rode the bike out of town.

Troy got to the next town. He hoped to get a job. He lived on the streets for days.

Troy ran out of food. He sold the bike for food money.

Troy walked the streets. He watched for the police. Did his foster mom call them? He slept in a park at night.

The town had no jobs. Troy knew he had to go. But he did not want to go back. Where to go next?

One day, he saw a passing train. It was going to the big city. Troy hopped onto the back of the train. He opened a door. He sat in the empty car.

Troy knew he had to go. And he did not look back.

STREET MEET

Troy made it to the big city. He lived on the streets for a few days.

He rode the city train at night. He slept there. It was safer than the streets.

But soon he ran out of money.

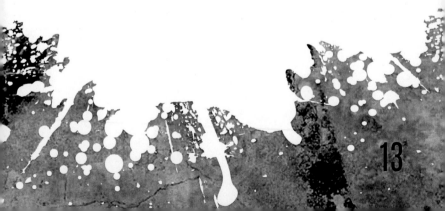

Troy walked the streets during the day. He began to beg for money. The downtown streets were busy. People were going to work. He found a street corner. It was *his* spot. He begged for money. He got some to buy food.

He had a lot of time to think. He liked being alone. But how long could he do this? Could he find a job? Could he find a place to live?

A young man walked up to Troy. He looked dirty. But he seemed happy. *Is he homeless too?* Troy wondered. Troy did not want to talk to him.

"What's up?" the young man said.

Troy said nothing. He looked the other way.

"Hey, you got any change?"

Troy said nothing.

"Hey, you are new here," the young man said. "I've never seen you before."

Troy could smell him. He smelled like booze.

"Hey, you got any change?" the young man said again.

Troy was getting mad.

"Do you talk?" the young man said.

Troy turned to him. He looked him in the eyes. "See this cup in my hand?" Troy asked. "Do you think I have change for you?"

The young man started to laugh. "He talks! I knew you could talk."

Troy smiled. *This dude is crazy,* Troy said to himself.

"Dude, I don't want your money. I'm just playing."

"Cool," Troy said.

16

"I'm Justin."

"I'm Troy."

They shook hands.

"See you later," Justin said. "I've got a date." He laughed.

Troy smiled.

TAKE SHELTER

A few days had gone by. Troy had not seen Justin. Was he okay? Troy hoped to see him again.

The days were getting colder. Winter was coming soon. Troy was still on the streets. He was still at his spot. He was still asking for money.

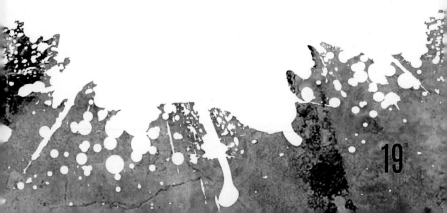

A woman walked past Troy. She was well dressed. She was going to work. She put some coins in Troy's cup.

"Thank you," Troy said.

The woman smiled and walked away. Then she turned and walked back. "It's cold out here," she said. "Do you use the shelter?"

"What shelter?" Troy asked.

"It's down the street," she said. "It's only a few blocks away. They can help you."

"Thanks," Troy said.

Troy did not know about the shelter. Did he want to go? Would they ask about his past? Or could he make it alone? Could he make it through the winter?

Troy walked the downtown streets. He found the shelter and walked in. There was a man at the door.

"Do you have any room?" Troy asked.

"What's your name, son?" the man asked.

"Troy."

"How old are you, Troy?" the man asked.

Troy stopped. He had to think fast. "Twenty," Troy said.

"I don't think so," the man said. "Do you have an ID?"

"No. I don't have one."

"This is an adult shelter. You have to prove your age or know someone here." The man gave Troy a card. "Go to this other shelter. The address is on the card. They take minors."

Troy did not want to go there. It was too far away. It was too far from his spot.

The front door opened. Justin came in. He saw Troy.

"Hey, man!" Justin said.

Troy was happy to see him.

"You know this guy?" the man asked Justin.

"Sure I do. He's my cousin."

Troy smiled at the man.

"Your cousin?" the man said. "What's his name?"

Troy looked at Justin. Justin looked at Troy. Justin stopped smiling. Could he think of Troy's name? They only met one time.

"Troy," Justin said. "He's my cousin, Troy."

Troy smiled again.

The man looked at both of them. "Okay," the man said to Justin. "He can stay. But you can't."

"Come on," Justin said. "Why not?"

"You know the rules," the man said. "You broke the rules."

"I will watch him," Troy said. "Can he stay if I watch him?"

The man looked at Troy. Then he looked at Justin. "One more fight and you are out," the man said. "Out for good."

TIME TO DIE

It was a getting cold outside. Troy still begged for money. He slept in the shelter at night. Sometimes the shelter was full. Troy slept in the park on those nights.

Some nights, he saw Justin in the park. Some nights, he saw Justin at the shelter.

One night, Troy saw Justin at the shelter. Justin had a black eye.

"Are you okay?" Troy asked. "Who did that to you?"

"Don't worry about it," Justin said. "It's cool."

The shelter door opened. A big guy came in. He looked like a football player. And he looked mean. Very mean. People on the street called him Big Man.

Big Man sat on a bed next to Justin.

"You got it yet?" Big Man asked Justin.

Troy did not speak.

"Did you hear me?" Big Man asked Justin. "I want my money."

"I told you. I don't have it."

Big Man stood up. He pulled out a knife.

Justin did not look at him.

Justin and Troy stood up. There was no time to think.

Big Man ran up to Justin. "You're dead," he said. He pushed the knife into Justin. The knife dug into Justin's gut. Big Man drew out the knife.

Troy pulled them apart. Justin fell back onto his bed.

Troy did not have time to think. Troy kicked the knife from Big Man's hand. The knife flew and hit the floor.

Troy punched Big Man. Big Man's back slammed against the wall.

Troy picked up the knife. He threw it at Big Man. The knife cut Big Man's ear. Then it got stuck in the wall.

Big Man ran at Troy. Troy kicked him hard. Big Man fell to the floor. He was in pain.

Troy was in shock. How did he do that?

Big Man got up and ran. He stopped at the shelter door. "You are both dead," he said. Then he ran out.

Troy turned to Justin. Justin was bleeding. Blood was all over the sheets. Troy took some sheets. He pressed them against Justin. It helped stop the bleeding.

"I owe you one," Justin said.

"We will see about that," Troy said. He smiled.

A shelter worker came into the room. "What the hell?" he said. He ran to a phone.

PARK KILLER

Justin went to the hospital. He was okay. The wound was not deep.

Troy thought Justin was a fun guy. He was funny. He made Troy laugh. Times were hard for Troy. He needed to laugh. Justin liked to have a good time.

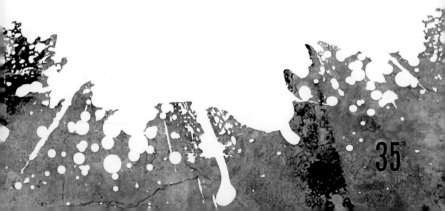

Troy was outside the shelter one cold day. Justin came up from behind. He held a toy water gun. He put it on Troy's back.

"Freeze!" Justin said. "Give me your money."

Troy knew it was Justin.

"What money?" Troy asked. Troy turned and they laughed.

Justin pointed the gun up. He aimed it at a bird. A bird on a fence. "Think I can't hit him?" Justin asked. "Bet you ten bucks I can."

"You are crazy, dude," Troy said. "Let's get inside. Before all the beds are gone."

"Wait," Justin said. He shot water at his face. "I've got to clean up first." Justin wiped the water from his face. Troy shook his head and smiled.

Winter was hard. Many more people found the shelter. The shelter filled up. Troy could not get in some nights.

One night, Troy was in the shelter. He watched for Justin. Justin never came.

There was a man in the next bed. "Did you hear?" he asked Troy.

"Hear what?"

"They are cutting the shelter's hours."

"What?" Troy asked.

"And the meals," the man said.

"Why?"

"They lost their funding," he said. "They may have to close."

Troy was mad. "They can't do that!" Troy yelled.

"Sure they can. Who cares about us?"

Troy sat up in his bed. What was he going to do? There was another shelter. It was on the other side of town. It only took in women and kids.

"Hey," the man said to Troy. "Did you hear?"

Troy was busy thinking.

"Did you hear?" he asked Troy again. "The park killer."

"What killer?" Troy asked.

"The park killer. It's the word on the street. Two people are dead. Two nights in a row."

"Are the cops looking?" Troy asked.

The man laughed. "They *say* they are looking. Why would they look? Two homeless people are dead. Why do they care?"

Justin, Troy said to himself. *Where is Justin?*

FINDING JUSTIN

Days passed. Troy had not seen Justin. There was a killer in the city. The cops were still looking. The killer was still out there. Two more homeless people were dead. They had been living under a bridge. Their bodies were found there.

Troy looked for Justin every night. He walked the streets. He looked in bars. He looked in the park.

He saw a guy in the park. Troy knew him. His name was Mike.

Mike had a spot deep in the park. It was next to an old shed. Mike slept in two sleeping bags. He made a fort. It was made out of shopping carts. Mike lived in the fort.

"Have you seen Justin?" Troy asked Mike.

"I saw him last night," Mike said. "He's trippin'."

"Why?" Troy asked.

"He thinks the killer is after him."

Big Man, Troy said to himself. "Where did Justin go?" Troy asked.

"I don't know," Mike said. "Justin moves. He never stays in one spot."

"Thanks," Troy said. Troy began to walk away.

"Wait," Mike said. Troy turned back. "Justin said one more thing."

"What?" Troy asked.

"He thinks the killer is after you too."

IN THE DARK

The next night was colder. It was going to snow. The shelter was full again. It would be closing soon. That was the word on the street.

More people were sleeping outside. They were all cold.

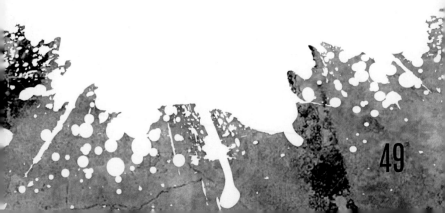

Troy kept looking for Justin. He found
two men in the park. They had built a
campfire. It felt warm.

"Are they hiring?" one man asked the
other.

"Next week," the other man said. "But
nobody knows yet. My brother works
there. He told me."

Troy stood there. He said nothing.

"Are you going?" the man asked.

"No," the other man said. "I'm too old for
that."

"Where is it?" Troy asked them.

"On West Adams Street," said one man.
"It's on the other side of town."

"What's the name of it?"

"Parker Meats," the other man said.
"Why? You think they will hire you?"

They were talking about a plant. A meat
packing plant. The plant was on the other
side of town.

"Maybe," Troy said. "Why not?" He
looked at the fire.

"You'll have a long walk, son." The men
laughed at Troy.

Troy put his hands close to the fire. He had to think. About many things. Big Man was out there. Was he the park killer? Where was Justin? Was he safe?

Troy rubbed his hands and kept thinking. He hated the streets. He hated the cold. He hated living in fear. He was done with all of it.

Could he get that job? Could he get off the streets? Could he go back to school?

Troy looked up. Somebody was coming. The other men looked up too. It was dark and hard to see. The person walked closer.

"Hold it!" one of the men said. "Stop where you are."

The person came even closer.

"We're not messing around," the other man said. "Stop where you are."

The person was very close.

Troy began to sweat. Was it the park killer? Was it Big Man?

TIME TO GO

Troy and the men were still. They stood around the fire. Troy's heart was pounding. Someone was out there. They were out there in the dark. And coming closer. Closer to the fire.

"Boo! Did I scare you?"

It was Justin. He stepped up to the fire. He held a bottle in his hand.

"I saw your faces. You were scared."
Justin laughed.

"Are you crazy?" one man asked.

"Yes," Troy said. "He is crazy."

"Hey, dude," Justin said. "You're trippin'.
Just relax. It's no big deal. Have a drink."

Justin handed Troy his bottle. Troy pushed
the bottle away. He was mad.

"Relax?" Troy said. "What about the park killer? What about Big Man?"

"Big Man skipped town," Justin said.

"Skipped town? How do you know?"

"Somebody told me," Justin said.

Troy put his hands in the air. "That's it," Troy said. "I'm tired of this, dude. I'm sick of all this. The shelter. The streets. The cold. Big Man. This park killer crap." Troy rubbed his face. He looked at the fire. He was so tired.

"Relax, Troy," Justin said.

"No, dude. I'm done. I'm getting out of here."

"Out of here? Where are you going?" Justin asked.

"He's going after that job," one man said.

"Job?" Justin asked. "What job? Troy, where are you going?"

Troy put out his hand.

Justin looked at Troy's hand. Then he shook it. Justin could not talk.